Contents

For my 'BOOKLARK' colleagues:-
Audrey Abel-Smith
Eleanor Fidler
Sue Goudie
Christine Kloet
Sheila Richardson
Kathleen Ryan
Derrick Scott
Margaret Sumner
Muriel Wills

1
A Ghost is Born

'What your Aunt Ivy needs is a ghost,' said Lenny Hargreaves to his friend, Jake Allen. 'That would pack the customers in.'

The two boys were slumped at a circular white table in the otherwise empty Ivy Tea Garden, miles from anywhere. All around them rolled acres of beautiful countryside, peopled solely by sheep.

The boys had previously spent a fortnight in

the country at Lenny's gran's, and both had enjoyed that very much. But then, Lenny's gran had a car and a sense of humour, and there had been other kids to play with in the village. Here, two miles from the nearest village of Bottlecombe, there was no one except Jake's widowed Aunt Ivy who had never been known to see the funny side of anything.

When he was first told that Jake's Aunt Ivy ran a tea garden, Lenny had visions of helping with mountains of washing-up. Once he had been assured that careful Aunt Ivy would never let him near her precious crockery, his mind then turned upon the interesting crowds of customers, for whom he could maybe put on magic shows while Jake took round the hat.

'I'm packing *all* my magic stuff,' Lenny told Jake, 'even the Vanishing Accomplice's special velvet curtain.' Since Lenny's dad, who was a long-distance lorry-driver, meant to transport them to Aunt Ivy's, there would be plenty of room for luggage. What could Jake do but sigh with resignation?

However, things did not turn out as expected. This was already the third day of the boys' visit, and the only tea garden customer so far had been a solitary hiker drinking a glass of milk with his own sandwiches, whilst he sorted out how he'd come to lose his way.

One thing was certain; Aunt Ivy could not be blamed for the lack of business. She was a genius in the kitchen, baked all her own scrumptious bread, cakes and scones, made her own jam, kept the place as clean as an operating theatre and tended every flower in her beautiful garden as if it were the vital stitch in the Bayeux Tapestry. Lenny felt she really deserved to succeed.

'It's a wonder your Aunt Ivy hasn't gone bankrupt. This place is too far off the beaten track,' mumbled Lenny, biting into a home-made raspberry tart with crispy, golden pastry. 'The main road must be three miles away. When you're whizzing down that at seventy miles an hour you're not going to stop for a two-foot strip of cockeyed board that says IVY TEA GARDEN NEXT LEFT.' He licked a stray blob of raspberry from his finger as he added:

'It's a rotten shame, this place going to waste. It needs a gimmick. Something to draw the crowds. Now, if that sign had a big, white picture of a ghost, and said HAUNTED IVY TEA GARDEN....'

Jake sighed with exasperation. 'All you'd do with a ghost would be to scare Aunt Ivy off. She'd close the place down and go and live somewhere else.'

10

'Not if she started making a fortune. Did you ever meet a grown-up who wasn't interested in making money? Anyway, she'd know the ghost story wasn't true. She'd just keep quiet and rake in the cash.'

'You don't know my Aunt Ivy. She has a conscience. She feels guilty if she thinks she's forgotten to say good morning to the cat.'

Lenny Hargreaves rolled his eyes and

sighed. 'All right; she needn't even know. As long as we convince other people. We'll simply start a rumour that this place is haunted.'

'And just how do you think you're going to manage that?'

'Easy!' retorted Lenny after only the slightest hesitation. 'All we need is a big black umbrella—like that tatty-looking man's-size thing I saw in the hallstand. Then—you remember my "Digits in the Dark" trick?'

'The one where you have those painted numbers on a bit of black cloth and they glow when you turn out the light?'

'That's it! Well, all we have to do is open the umbrella and paint a face on it with that glowing paint. Then when it's dark we stick the umbrella out of our bedroom window and keep opening and shutting it. Anybody passing will think they're seeing a ghost, appearing and disappearing.'

'You reckon?' grinned Jake, entirely unconvinced. 'Well, there must be at least two people walking past here every week.'

'Alternatively,' Lenny cut in nastily, 'we

could just sit around here for the next fortnight and die slowly of overeating.'

There was a long, sulky silence. Then Jake unfolded his arms and said, 'Well, it's your idea, so you can go and ask for the umbrella.'

The paint-pot in Lenny's conjuring outfit was not very big. In fact, it looked more like an outsize meat-paste jar. Still, Lenny reckoned there was enough paint in it for a sizeable face. He cleared a space on the floor of the junk-filled garage, opened the umbrella and set to work, tongue sticking out and eyes screwed up in concentration. But Lenny Hargreaves was no artist, and the face took on a crazy, cross-eyed look which set Jake Allen laughing. Once Jake started he couldn't stop. He was soon lurching about the garage in helpless hysterics. He lurched so wildly that he collided with Lenny, who tripped over a rusty watering-can and spilt the paint all over the umbrella, completely covering up the face. Making a desperate grab, he tipped the umbrella over, so that the paint ran on to the inside as well.

Lenny was absolutely furious. 'Now look what you've done!'

'Well, honestly, if you could have seen. . . .'

'You've ruined everything now. There's no paint left.'

Jake sobered up. 'So what? No need to get so steamy. We can open and shut the umbrella just the same. It will look like a moving shiny blur from a distance, and that's just as ghostly. In fact, believe me, it'll be a lot more ghostly than that crummy face you painted.'

Lenny pretended to look hurt, but he was bound to admit that Jake was right. He only wished he had thought of the moving shiny blur himself in the first place. Still, the haunting was his idea. Any fool could mess about with the minor details of a plan, but the basic stroke of genius was what really mattered.

'Yeah, maybe it will work. We'll give it a try.'

''Course it will work. You just need to start people's imaginations off, and let them do the rest. You'd be surprised what eye-witnesses think they've seen.'

'You've changed your tune, haven't you?'

'Let's just say your enthusiasm is catching.'

'You realise we'll have to stay awake until midnight? That's when ghosts are supposed to show.'

'What if nobody is around to see it? That's the main problem.'

'There's a full moon tonight. With a bit of luck that umbrella will be visible all the way to Bottlecombe.'

'Well, if we have to stay up late we'll get Aunt Ivy to play Scrabble. It takes her at least half an hour to work out every move. I've known one game to last a fortnight.'

Lenny groaned. If there was one game he hated it was Scrabble. Too much like school, for one thing.

'All right, then. Leave the umbrella open to dry. We'll pick it up at bedtime.'

'The Haunted Ivy Tea Garden,' mused Jake experimentally.

'Sound great! If I was a sight-seer and I'd just heard about it, I'd be off there like a shot!' declared Lenny Hargreaves.

2
The Ghost Vanishes

During the evening a wind arose. The Scrabble game was punctuated by strange howlings under doors and inside chimneys, and a tree outside the kitchen window swung in growing frenzy against the glass. Perfect weather for ghosts!

Inside the house, the evening passed pleasantly enough, though spelling was evidently not Aunt Ivy's strong point. Lenny felt cheered

17

to find that there were other people as baffled by the English language as he was. Jake, on the other hand, had a flair for spelling and made the most of it. None of this turning soft and letting the others win a game, just to keep them happy. Yet for once Lenny Hargreaves did not mind losing. He had his haunting to look forward to.

By the time the boys went off to bed it was almost eleven o'clock. Swift, black clouds chased over the moon, leaving only occasional patches of light.

'You go upstairs and start making a noise in the bathroom,' whispered Lenny, 'whilst I nip round to the garage to collect the umbrella.'

It would never do for Aunt Ivy to guess what they were up to.

But when Lenny reached the garage, he had his first shock of the evening. The umbrella was not there. At first he thought Aunt Ivy had closed it up and tossed it among the other junk. Or had she put it back in the hallstand? After a great deal of frenzied searching, Lenny stormed upstairs.

'All right, what have you done with it?'

It turned out that Jake had moved the umbrella outside the garage door, to help it dry more quickly in the fresh air.

'Fresh air's right, you nutcase! Only it happens to be a force ten gale. That umbrella's probably blown to Timbuctoo by now.'

'Well, it was a crack-brained scheme to start with.'

'You're useless, you know that?'

'At least I can *spell*.'

'Big deal!' grunted Lenny, climbing disgustedly into bed without even cleaning his teeth.

Halfway to a dream, however, he was roused again by a frantic knocking downstairs. Aunt

Ivy had a customer!

'Hear that?' Both boys sat up in bed.

'It's after midnight. Something must be up!' United by a crisis, they were instantly friends again. As one, they leapt out of bed and rushed to listen on the landing.

Aunt Ivy, who had just been locking up before retiring for the night, was now unbolting the front door again, though she kept it on the chain as she peered through the gap and asked who was there.

'It's me, Dave Doyle!' a man's voice called. 'Do you mind if I come in and use your 'phone?'

'He's from the farm up the lane,' whispered Jake. 'His own 'phone must be out of order. Perhaps the lines have blown down.'

'Well, he's no need to make such a noise about it.' Lenny was thinking wistfully that here would have been the perfect ghost-spotter, if only they hadn't gone and lost the ghost. How maddening! He was about to trail disappointedly back to bed when he had the third shock of the evening, hearing what Dave Doyle was saying as Aunt Ivy let him in:

'Have you seen it? Isn't it amazing? I couldn't believe my eyes, honestly. I just stood and stared at it like somebody daft. Going to ring the papers right away, before it's out of sight. They pay you for stories like this, you know, and by the time I get home it could be gone.'

'What could be gone? What are you talking about?' Aunt Ivy followed Dave to the telephone, sniffing suspiciously at his breath, but she did not learn any more until he had dialled his number.

'*Bottlecombe Bugle*? Dave Doyle here, Lane End Farm. I've got a scoop for you if you're interested. There's a FLYING SAUCER hovering over the Ivy Tea Garden right this minute. No, not sorcerer; *saucer*. As in tea-set. No, I haven't been celebrating. If you must know, I've been to a Temperance Meeting. All right, if you don't believe me, grab your binoculars, walk outside and look up!'

Jake and Lenny waited to hear no more. Despite the fierce wind, they flung open the landing window and thrust their heads out into the night. The wind was deafening. Dustbin lids and milk bottles bowled around the back garden, whilst from further afield came louder bangs and rattles, as gates, sheds and fences took the strain. The boys were just in time to see a curved silver shape disappearing swiftly but gracefully behind the farthest clump of trees in the nearby wood.

'Our umbrella!'

'Fancy thinking that was a flying saucer!'

'I told you folks would believe anything!'

'Even ghosts, then.'

'Yeah, what a waste!'

'Oh, I dunno! This could be a stroke of luck.' Lenny began dragging Jake back into the bedroom. 'This could turn out as good as any ghost. If the flying saucer tale gets into the papers, everybody will want to come and look at the place. And while they're looking they can be stuffing themselves with your Aunt Ivy's coffee and scones.'

'Huh! There won't be much of a story left when they find that umbrella!'

'They're not *going* to find it!' Lenny was already scrambling into his clothes.

3
Spirited Away

Jake and Lenny stood on the edge of the wood and peered into the blackness. 'It can't be in there,' grumbled Jake. 'It would never have come down through all those trees.'

'Well, it's not on the outside of the wood, either. Must have caught on a treetop.'

'It might have taken off again. Didn't somebody mention Timbuctoo?'

'No, it didn't take off again. We'd have seen

it. It's around here somewhere.'

'All right, let's walk back up the fields in case we missed it.' Jake suddenly stopped and held out his hand. ''Course, it would blooming-well start to rain!'

Lenny was growing crosser every minute. The loss of the umbrella was all Jake Allen's fault, yet the lad did nothing but grumble and complain. The final straw came when Lenny's torchlight suddenly flickered and died.

'Huh! That's all we need! Here, shine your torch this way, so I can see what's up with mine.'

'Needs a new battery, that's all. Didn't you bring any spares?'

Lenny fiddled about with his torch wondering if it might help to bonk Jake on the head with it. Now Jake would have to be leader. As if that wasn't bad enough, it was Jake who suddenly claimed to have spotted the umbrella.

'Look! It *is* in the wood, after all.'

Certainly there was a round, shiny shape bobbing merrily about among the trees. Was it their umbrella? Lenny could hardly believe it.

'How did it get in there?'

'Perhaps it blew in along the ground. Let's grab it before it blows away again.' Stabbing his torch into the darkness, Jake leapt in among the trees, leaving Lenny to stumble and blunder behind him.

It was incredible how difficult the going suddenly became. There were roots and tangles everywhere, and long, sharp, nasty twigs that tried to scratch the boys' eyes out. Every step required concentration; it was no use trying to hurry. Even at the slowest pace, there were untold hazards. At one point, Jake caught his foot in a rabbit hole and stumbled forward on to hands and knees. The torch flew from his grasp and rolled down a bank, where it settled snugly into a clump of bracken. A good thing the beam of light was uppermost, to guide Lenny to where it lay. When Lenny came back from his scramble down the bank, he found Jake hopping crazily up and down.

'I've lost my shoe.'

'How have you managed that?'

'It came off when I fell.'

'You prize idiot! Why didn't you stand still, then, until you found it? Now you've gone hopping about all over the place we'll never know where it is. Here, let me look.'

Lenny shone the torch around in all directions, but there was no sign of the shoe.

'Whereabouts were you when you fell?'

Lenny had lost his own bearings because of the scramble after the torch, and all Jake knew was that it was most uncomfortable to put his shoeless foot down on the prickly wet ground. As for the umbrella, they had now lost sight of that completely.

'Oh, let's pack it in! We'll come back in the daylight.'

'Somebody else could have found the umbrella by then.'

'So what? Nobody's going to believe that tale anyway. I'll bet the *Bugle* editor's laughing his head off this very minute.'

'You were the one who said folks believed anything.'

'That was before I lost my shoe.'

Lenny sighed, suddenly realising how tired he was, not to mention scratched, wet through and fed up. 'Can you make it home with only one shoe?'

'I'll manage. But my mum's not going to be overjoyed at forking out for a new pair.' Wearily they turned in what they thought was the right direction for Aunt Ivy's. But they were in for a shock. The tiny pathway suddenly seemed to peter out, and the trees had grown ominously darker and closer together. Feeling uneasy, the boys forged anxiously ahead, getting ever more tangled in the thickening undergrowth. Half an hour later, they had to admit they were lost.

Meantime, at the Ivy Tea Garden, the excitement was building up. Mr Grubb, the *Bugle* editor himself, arrived by car, having insisted that Dave Doyle should wait for him there, on the spot where he had sighted his saucer, rather than go rushing off home.

'Now then, Dave, what sort of a tale is this supposed to be?' Mr Grubb looked decidedly

sceptical, though he had his notebook with him all the same.

'Didn't you see it? I know it sounds crazy; *I* couldn't believe it either, but it was there all right.'

'It was probably a plane you saw, or a helicopter.'

'Too low; far too low.'

'Maybe it was in trouble. We could 'phone the police and see if there's been a crash in the area.'

'We'd have heard a crash,' insisted Dave

quite crossly. 'Anyway, I tell you it wasn't a plane. It was round. A proper circle. Looked more like a giant frisbee than anything.'

'Now, let's not get carried away,' cautioned Mr Grubb, trying hard not to smile. 'Facts, we want, not wild flights of fancy.' He turned to Aunt Ivy. 'Didn't *you* see anything?'

Aunt Ivy had to admit that she had just caught a glimpse of something silver disappearing over the treetops as she opened the front door, but surely to goodness it could not have been a flying saucer? There were no such things.

'I wouldn't be too sure about that if I were you,' Dave said darkly. He had just been reading a book by an American who claimed to have talked to two Venusians in some desert or other. 'If we can reach the moon, then why shouldn't other beings get to us?'

Mr Grubb surveyed the night sky carefully. 'Well, there's nothing up there now except a load of rain-clouds. We'll leave it until the morning and see if any reports turn up from elsewhere.'

'That means you don't believe me. Well, you'll be sorry. When did your paper last have a decent bit of news in it?'

'Why don't we all have a nice cup of tea?' offered Aunt Ivy, trying to keep the peace. She began arranging crockery and biscuits on a tray.

'Just a quick one, then.' The editor looked at his watch, reminding himself that he still had that morning's stamp and postal-order snatch at Bottlecombe Post Office to write up.

There was a piece of news, all right! Mr Grubb intended to give it a whole front page spread. That would make Dave Doyle eat his words, and no mistake!

It was as Aunt Ivy was crossing the hall with the teapot that she noticed a strong draught blowing in from the staircase. The landing window was open! Strange. She could not remember opening it, and surely the boys would never do such a thing on a windy night like this? Having delivered the tray to her guests, she went off upstairs to investigate. First she closed the landing window. Then she

noticed that the door to the boys' room was open. She peeped inside—and found them gone! Their beds had been slept in, but the boys were not there. Alarmed, she dashed from room to room, finding no trace of the boys except a dirty sock on top of the bathroom cabinet. Finally she burst in upon her guests with the shocking news that her nephew and his friend had vanished!

The editor's whole face lit up like a Christmas tree.

This was more like it! A real, down-to-earth mystery that could share the front page with the Post Office drama. Two good stories in one edition; it had never been known before. Mr Grubb whipped out his notebook again and started firing questions; Aunt Ivy was distraught.

'You don't suppose it has anything to do with—what Dave was saying?'

Into her mind swam a picture of the boys being spirited away through the landing window by some fantastic machine belonging to aliens from outer space. Crazy, the way your imagination ran away with itself when you panicked. She could now understand Dave's story much better than she had done half an hour ago.

'I'm sure there's a simple explanation,' soothed Mr Grubb, hoping otherwise. 'Best thing we can do is to search around outside. Then, when we're sure they're not just hiding or playing a game, we'll get on to the police.'

'Police?' shrieked Aunt Ivy.

'Only to help us search a bit quicker. They

know how to set about these things properly.'

'It's all my fault!' Aunt Ivy wailed. 'I should have made sure the landing window was locked. I should have. . . .'

'There, there!' Mr Grubb gave Aunt Ivy's shoulder a consoling pat. 'I'm sure it will all end happily.' As far as he was concerned it would, for he had just thought of a wonderful headline: MISSING BOYS IN UFO MYSTERY. It was the best thing that had happened to him in years.

4
Hole in the Ground

'I'm not going any further,' declared Jake Allen, standing on one leg with his weight against a tree. The sock on his shoeless foot now had more holes in it than a hairnet.

'I don't blame you. It's bad enough with two shoes on.' Lenny's own two shoes were packed with mud, inside and out.

'We'll have to sit here until daylight, rain or no rain. I refuse to fight my way through any

more branches.'

'I'll have a scout around. There must be a bit of shelter somewhere. Lend me your torch a minute.'

'Not likely! You're not going off and leaving me in the dark.'

'Don't be so soft! What are you scared of—a pack of ravening wolves, or the Abominable Snowman?'

'Suppose that bobbing shape we saw wasn't the umbrella after all? We never caught up with it. It just seemed to disappear.'

'Oh, come on! You don't think it was a real ghost, do you?'

'It's all right for you. I can't even run away, my foot's so blooming sore.'

'You won't have to run away. I'll only be gone two minutes.' Lenny took the torch and swung it in a wide arc, peering hopefully into the night.

At last he called: 'There's a great slab of rock over there. I'll just see if we can crawl in underneath it.'

'Don't go and get stuck or anything.'

Lenny shuffled off and returned almost immediately with the news that he had found a neat little hollow. 'Like a sort of cave. It'll be great. There's a big slab of rock to sit on, and an even bigger one hanging over it to keep us dry. It's even got creepers hanging down like curtains in front of it. Come on, I'll show you.'

Jake hobbled after his friend, and was relieved to find that Lenny's promise was true. He sat down with a sigh of exhaustion. 'I couldn't have gone another step.'

'Not exactly five-star,' admitted Lenny, 'but it will have to do until morning.'

'I hope Aunt Ivy hasn't missed us, that's all.

She'll go frantic if she has.'

'She'll be snoring away by now.'

'I wish I was. You and your dratted ghost.'

'If you hadn't left that umbrella outside. . . .'

'And if you hadn't brought your magic stuff on holiday, especially that crummy luminous paint . . . .'

They went on sniping at each other, with less and less energy and conviction, until both of them fell asleep.

It was almost two in the morning by the time Constable Waddle arrived at Aunt Ivy's on his bicycle. The constable had not managed more than ten minutes' break, he said, since the Post Office drama, so he was not feeling too good-tempered. The garden and surrounding fields had been searched by Dave Doyle and Mr Grubb, but the boys had not been found. Aunt Ivy was in a state of great agitation.

'Can't do much till daylight,' pronounced the constable. 'It would be hopeless, groping round in the pitch dark and all this rain. It's only a couple of hours to dawn.'

'We can't wait for dawn!' Ivy cried in horror. 'Goodness knows what could happen to those poor boys while we're sitting here doing nothing.'

With a sigh, the constable began to explain the difficulties of setting up a search-party, and in fact, since there were two boys missing instead of one, he was not yet convinced the matter was urgent. They were probably off on some secret assignment of their own.

'I don't mind driving around for a bit,' Mr Grubb offered. 'I could go up as far as the edge of the moors. Just let me make another couple of 'phone calls first.'

He smirked with satisfaction as he thought of his sub-heading: ALL NIGHT MOORLAND SEARCH—EYE-WITNESS REPORT.

5
Bad News Travels Fast

The television van arrived soon after dawn. It pulled up outside the Ivy Tea Garden, blocking the narrow lane and looking totally out of place in such rural surroundings. Two young men emerged from it and stared thoughtfully over Aunt Ivy's garden wall. One of them consulted a clip-board, then walked up the path and rang the doorbell, whilst the other sat down on the wall and lit a slim cigar.

Minnie Doyle, Dave's wife, who had been summoned to keep Ivy company, opened the door.

The man with the clip-board said good morning and wondered if it were too early for breakfast.

'We're closed!' Minnie told him brusquely. She had been up all night and was feeling the effects. But before she could shut the door again, the man slipped his foot into the gap and beamed up a charming smile.

'This is Bottlecombe's Ivy Tea Garden, isn't it?'

'Can't you read, then?' Minnie had no time this morning for social niceties. She was concerned only with poor Ivy's welfare.

'We're investigating a couple of possible items for tonight's regional news programme, and of course we need to make an early start. I'm sure you won't mind if we. . . .'

'Oh, yes I will mind! We aren't open to nobody today, not even if the Queen herself was to ask, so you can just go and do your investigating somewhere else.'

The man found this an unusual reception. Most people were only too keen to get themselves on to a news programme. Still, nothing daunted, he raised a hand to the second man, who rose from the wall and joined him. Introductions followed. Minnie heard the men's names as Jostling and Orbury, and was not impressed by the smoke from the slim cigar, which she wafted vigorously aside.

'Just a couple of questions, that's all,' smiled Orbury through his smoke haze. 'Then maybe two or three shots of the place. . . .'

'Shots, is it? Well, let me tell you my dad's the gamekeeper in these parts, and if there's any shooting to be done, he'll do it. If you're not off this doorstep in ten seconds flat. . . .'

Orbury, to his great disappointment, was never to savour the full richness of Minnie's threat, for at that moment Aunt Ivy herself appeared in the doorway, haggard and haunted-looking, but as gentle-voiced as ever.

'It's a bit early for sitting outside, but if you'd like to come into the kitchen I'll make you some coffee in a minute. Then I could do you ham, eggs, tomatoes, toast and marmalade.'

Minnie was indignant. 'Ivy, you can't!'

'Why not? Life must go on. I'd rather keep busy until the searchers get back, and anyway these gentlemen may be able to help. If they put it out on the news that the boys are missing, maybe somebody, somewhere. . . .'

Tears rushed into Aunt Ivy's eyes and she could say no more. Minnie flew protectively towards her, at the same time rounding on the intruders. 'Now look what you've done! You ought to be ashamed of yourselves. You're worse than them newspaper folk, and that's saying something.'

Both men began to apologise at once. 'We didn't know anything about missing boys.'

'You'll have to forgive me,' Aunt Ivy smiled bravely. 'I know the boys will turn up soon with some simple explanation. Boys that age are full of mischief, especially our Jake's friend. It's just the waiting—and all these funny rumours.'

'Ah, yes!' Jostling hoisted his clip-board. 'That's what really brought us along. These rumours. Somebody is supposed to have spot-

ted a UFO, I believe?'

Minnie gave Ivy a gentle push towards the house. 'You go and see to the breakfasts, then. I'll deal with the rumours.'

As soon as Ivy was out of earshot, Minnie spoke sharply to the men.

'Can't you see she's upset? You don't want to go making things worse for the poor soul. The policeman's got a search-party going, so why don't you set off after them? They've only just left here, and they're heading for the woods.'

'We really wanted to talk to an eye-witness about this UFO.'

'That's my husband, Dave Doyle. He's gone off with the search-party. You can't miss him; he's wearing a blue anorak and a blue corduroy cap. He'll tell you a tale, all right. In fact, you'll have a job to stop him. You can believe him, an' all, for he hasn't the brains to make up a tale like that. If he says he saw a flying saucer, then he saw one.'

Jostling looked at Orbury. 'What do you think?'

Orbury shrugged. 'Not much doing at all,

I'd say. Maybe the missing boys are worth a line or two. Couple of shots of the search-party, something like that. After breakfast, of course.'

'Odds are these boys will have turned up again by then, so we won't be able to use the story.'

'Oh, you never know your luck!' smiled Orbury hopefully.

6
A Strange Apparition

Lenny Hargreaves woke up with a start. Something small and furry had just run over his foot. Heart beating fast, he fought a double battle with his memory and his cold, stiff limbs, as he tried to scramble to his knees. Then it all came back to him; the umbrella, the search, the lost shoe and the hiding-place.

'Hey, Jake! Wake up, it's coming daylight! We can try to find our way back now.'

'Uh?' Jake rolled over sleepily, then suddenly started groaning. 'Ooooh, I think I've got rheumatics, like my grandad.'

'Now we know what the chickens feel like in the deep freeze.'

'I'll never walk again.'

"Course you will! You just need to get your circulation going.' As they crawled out of their hiding-place they saw immediately that the wood by daylight was a much friendlier place. The rain had stopped, the birds were singing, early sunlight filtered sideways through the trees.

'Try this!' Lenny began swinging his arms and running on the spot, but Jake's effort looked more like a limping gorilla. When they had limbered up sufficiently, they took stock of their surroundings.

'Which way do you think we should go?'

'Haven't a clue! Unless—wait a minute! That's my shoe over there!'

Jake lumbered forward to gather up this soggy object, whilst Lenny groaned in disgust. 'We must have gone right round in circles then,

last night.'

Jake thrust his toes into the shoe. 'Ugh! I think there's mushrooms growing in it.' He tipped up the shoe and shook it. A leaf fell out, then a small, black, squashy lump. 'That's better! Now let's get back home. I'm starving.'

'Yeah, three-and-a-half cheers for breakfast! I'll have four eggs, five rashers of bacon, six sausages, eight rounds of toast and ten cups of tea,' Lenny threatened.

'By then it will be time for elevenses. Hot buttered scones with raspberry jam, raisin pancakes, cream buns and coffee.'

'No, milk-shakes.'

'Hey—I've just remembered something. It's apple crumble day!'

Spurred on by the thought of all this food, the boys made splendid progress through the wood. They soon found the path again, and were nearing the stile that would lead over the last fence into the fields beyond when Lenny halted, staring goggle-eyed before him.

'Look at that!'

'What is it?'

'Looks like—a FLYING SAUCER!'

The boys gazed spellbound into the field beyond, where a great silver upturned basin sat strangely upon the grass. It was big enough to mix an omelette that would feed five thousand folks.

'We're not dreaming, are we?'

'You pinch me, and I'll pinch you.'

'Dave Doyle was right, then. What he saw was nothing to do with our umbrella.'

'Looks like it.'

'Hey—don't you think it's a bit spooky?' asked Jake.

51

Lenny grinned. 'It will be if we hear any little green men shouting, "Take me to your leader!" Apart from that, I'd say it's more interesting than anything. It's not every day you see a sight like this.'

'Intriguing, that's the word for it,' Jake offered, showing off.

'No kidding? I'll bet you can spell that, can't you?'

Lenny was already crossing the field towards the flying saucer, so of course Jake followed him, though he managed to keep well in the rear. He wasn't scared, he told himself; just cautious. Nobody could accuse Lenny Hargreaves of that.

Lenny stared hard at the object, taking in every detail. It seemed to be made of a sort of lightweight, shiny plastic, though of course it could be some special space-substance, never seen on earth before. Lenny willed it to be a genuine UFO, though well aware that Fate was rarely so obliging. Just suppose it were, though? What an adventure to tell when they got back to school—if they ever did!

The boys circled the saucer cautiously, discovering a broken place at one side of it, near to the base of the curve. (Had a meteor hit it?) So of course Lenny had to stick his head inside the hole.

'There's something in there, making a noise. Trying to communicate with us.'

'Sure to be!' sneered Jake, but his stomach gave a peculiar lurch and he looked round for a suitable weapon, just in case. There was a blown-down branch nearby, so he picked that up and tried a few martial arts manoeuvres. Lenny started laughing.

'You know what it is? It's a cat! Daft thing's jumped in and can't get out. We'll have to rescue it.'

'You're not going in?'

'I think I've a bit more sense than a cat.' Lenny had already put one foot through the gap.

'You haven't got nine lives.' Jake's imagination had filled with banks of computers, flashing lights and electronic beams. As for the actual life-forms that might be in there. . . !

Shouts and cat noises began to echo round the dome, and once or twice Lenny screeched with pain. At last he caught the animal and held it up towards the hole. 'Catch!'

The cat, thoroughly scared, writhed energetically in Lenny's grasp and finally leapt away, right over Jake's outstretched arms, to run off down the field as if all the Dogs of Mars were after it.

'Hasn't half scratched me!' complained Lenny, lifting red-streaked hands on to the edge of the gap. 'Here, help me out.'

'What's that you've got?' Jake was staring at a bundle of papers stuffed into the front of Lenny's anorak.

'Taped to the roof, these were. Secret documents from outer space. Wait till the *Bugle* editor casts an eye on this lot!'

'They're sheets of postage stamps!' Jake had noted the neatly-perforated edges. Lenny took out the bundle and examined it more carefully.

'You're right! Stamps—and postal orders!'

'Perhaps the Daleks do football pools,' sneered Jake, throwing down his stick.

7

A Whirlwind Solution

After a hearty breakfast, the two men in the television van drove off to look for the search-party, as Minnie Doyle had suggested.

'Follow this lane until you come to a gateway with a big pile of muck and a milk-churn. Then start walking across the fields.'

'Wild goose chase?' wondered Orbury after half a mile of muddy lane.

'Could be, in more ways than one.'

'Suppose we keep on, then, and do a piece on that sinking supermarket instead?'

This new resolve was strengthened when they turned a corner and saw just how big Minnie's pile of muck really was. They were so busy taking it in that they almost missed seeing the obstacle in their path. Jostling suddenly applied his brakes. Two grubby, wild young boys were rushing towards the van, waving frantically. Jostling wound down the window.

'Anything wrong?'

'Plenty!' panted Lenny Hargreaves. 'We've just found a flying saucer full of stamps and postal orders.'

Orbury groaned. 'Oh, not another flying saucer!'

Jostling climbed out of the van. 'Now, take a couple of deep breaths, calm down and start again. At the beginning.'

'You don't believe us, do you?'

'We're not surprised. Nobody ever believes a thing we say.'

'We're always right, as well. But by the time folks decide to take notice it's usually too late.'

59

'Did I say I didn't believe you? You haven't given me a chance.' Jostling sat down carefully on a bit of grass verge and motioned the boys to join him. Orbury came too.

'Now then, from the beginning.'

'Well, he has this conjuring outfit that a princess once gave him. It had some luminous paint in it, and we got this umbrella. . . .'

'We thought if there was a ghost more people would come, you see. . . .'

'Just a minute! What has all this to do with a flying saucer?'

'You said start at the beginning.'

'I meant start by telling who you are.'

Of course, the minute Jake and Lenny did that, Jostling realised they were the two missing boys from the Ivy Tea Garden. Without waiting to hear any more, he bundled the boys into the van. 'Come on! The sooner we put your auntie out of her misery the better.'

'But we haven't told you about the flying saucer yet.'

'All in good time.' Orbury glanced hopefully at his watch. Maybe they could fit in some early elevenses.

When she saw the boys, Aunt Ivy actually burst into tears, a phenomenon which Jake had never witnessed before. He found it quite gratifying to have been missed so badly, though he guessed that retribution would be on its way when his mum found out. 'Serve us right, too,' he thought, feeling sorry for the upset.

'Two hot baths and two big breakfasts, I should think!' Minnie Doyle was already rummaging in the fridge. Yet, hungry as they were, the boys could not bear the agony of remaining unbelieved.

'Please, Aunt Ivy, just let us show somebody the flying saucer first. We'll be right back.'

Lenny turned to Jostling. 'You could drive us there in five minutes. Would you?'

But by now Aunt Ivy had pulled herself together. Nothing would be allowed to take precedence over baths, clean clothes and at least a hot drink. What was more, Aunt Ivy had no intention of letting the boys out of her sight again just yet. If they went off in the van, then she was coming, too. So in the end, while

Minnie cleaned up the bath, put the boys' clothes to soak, and went to work on gigantic breakfast preparations, the rest of them drove in the van back to the spot where Jostling had picked up the boys.

'It's just down there!' Lenny pointed over a fence to the second field in view. Orbury thought he could just see the top of something silver gleaming in the sunlight. He reached for his camera.

Lenny took the lead, sprinting ahead in his eagerness to prove himself right. He had been anxious in case the saucer had flown, but he need not have worried. There it sat, exactly as before.

As soon as Aunt Ivy caught sight of the 'saucer' she could not help smiling. 'You know what that is? It's the top off the band-stand in Bottlecombe Park.'

'You what?'

'You mean—it blew off in the gale?'

'Then how do you account for these?' Lenny produced the wad of stamps and postal orders, which so far he had managed to keep hidden, having transferred them from one set of 'magic' pockets to another.

Everyone gathered round to look, and Aunt Ivy remembered that, according to Constable Waddle, a man in a stocking-mask had made off with all the stamps and postal orders from Bottlecombe Post Office yesterday morning. Quite a crowd of people had given chase, and the thief had fled across the park, where he finally disappeared among the trees.

'But not before he'd hidden his loot, it seems.'

'And *we* found it!'

'Hey, I'll bet I know where the thief is, as well. He's hiding in the woods. Remember that bobbing glow we saw last night?'

'If he is in there, the search-party will soon flush him out. So in a way, we'll have found *him* as well! Not bad eh, Jake?'

Orbury had been working on his camera, which he now hoisted on to his shoulder. 'Well, I think all this is worth a mention on the news. What say you, Jostling?'

Jostling waved his clip-board at Lenny.

'Back to that hole and peer into it, like you did the first time. That should make a good shot. And you, Jake; what were you doing at the time?'

'Wielding my trusty club. Like this.'

'Ow! Mind the camera! Right then, in a minute I'm going to start asking you some questions. Answer them clearly and slowly, and don't both start talking at once. . . .'

8
Ghost Garden

'We're on the telly!' Jake called to Minnie as they arrived back home. 'You'll be able to see us on tonight's news.'

'Good thing you had them baths, then.' Minnie began serving up a hearty meal.

'Pity the Tea Garden couldn't have been in the film, though,' grumbled Lenny. 'That's just the sort of publicity we were looking for. We seem to have done everything except what we set out to do, which was to put Aunt Ivy on the map.'

Jostling had to agree that it certainly was a lovely garden.

'Couldn't we take another shot or two, then—sort of, showing where the boy heroes live?'

'No,' said Orbury firmly. 'News has to be filmed as and where it happens. You can't go adding bits on for fun. It's got to be as genuine as possible.'

'In that case, Jake and I should still have been dirty and messed up.'

'Tell you what, though, Lenny—you've given me an idea!' Jostling looked suddenly excited, though his eye was on the boys, not the garden. Could they both be destined to end up slurping soup in some commercial? But Jostling would not be drawn. 'Needs pondering yet awhile. We'll let you know if anything comes of it. In fact, if anything does, we'll be back in a few days with a friend of ours.'

'I'll bet they will!' sneered Jake as the van finally drove away. 'They only said that to cheer us up.'

'Well, at least we had one good adventure, and your Aunt Ivy must have made a bit of profit out of all those breakfasts.'

'Not her! Do you know what she did? She fed all the searchers *free* on account of them looking for us.'

'I sometimes wonder if your Aunt Ivy really *wants* to get rich. It could be we're just wasting our time.'

Just then a distant commotion heralded the return of the search-party—with a prisoner. This, they proclaimed, was the Post Office thief, caught sheltering miserably in the woods under a strange-looking silver umbrella.

'Bet he pinched *that*, as well! Though we can't think where from.'

For the moment, Lenny and Jake felt it wiser to say nothing more, especially as Aunt Ivy had just promised to take them to Bottlecombe Fair on Saturday.

'Aren't you mad at us?' Lenny marvelled. He couldn't imagine his mum taking him to the fair after all the upset he'd caused. Life was full

of surprises.

It was certainly a surprise for Jake and Lenny to see themselves on television, for they looked like a couple of strangers.

'That's not really us, is it?' asked Jake, even further bemused by the name-tags which read JACOB ALLEN AND LEONARD HAR-GREAVES.

'Pity your Aunt Ivy hasn't a video-recorder. We need to get used to it.'

'Think yourself lucky you've seen it at all. She's only had her telly for six months. Before that, she just used to play Patience and crochet these wiggly yellow mats, and listen to "Woman's Hour" on the radio.'

'They've no business to go cutting bits out of the news, though. Especially after what Orbury said about trying to be genuine. You know when Jostling was interviewing me? I said all that about my conjuring, and none of it was in the programme. Not a word!'

'He's probably jealous.'

Friday seemed flat after all the excitement. Even Saturday's fair was a mixed blessing. Jake won a plastic frog for his baby sister, but Lenny lost forty pence on the 'roll-your-own-pennies'. Also, although the bumper cars were fun, the ghost train turned out to be a miserable fiasco. Sunday morning poured with rain, and the boys' mood was one of gloom. Yet had they but known it, Sunday was plump with surprises.

Just before lunch-time the rain stopped, the sun came out and a smart blue car drew up at Ivy's gate. Three men stepped out of it—Jostling, Orbury and their promised friend. The friend was a distinguished gentleman with white hair and expensive clothes, who gazed thoughtfully around him like someone completely new to fields and trees.

Jostling and Orbury waved as they came up the path. 'Told you we'd be back!'

'You only said you might.'

'Anyway, we didn't believe you,' Jake said frankly. 'People never do come back here.'

'They will!' Orbury winked at Jostling.

Aunt Ivy came out to greet her visitors and asked if they would stay to lunch.

'Yes, please. We'll take the table with the best view. We've brought Miles Pellington with us.'

('I hope they're going to pay,' whispered Lenny to Jake.)

It was obvious that Jostling expected the name Miles Pellington to cause a sensation, but however famous that gentleman might be in the television world, Aunt Ivy had clearly never heard of him. She simply fetched a cloth and began wiping up the rain from the best table-top.

'A beautiful spot you live in,' Miles told Ivy. 'Most photogenic bit of countryside I've seen for a long time.'

'I wouldn't live anywhere else.'

'Not even after all this scandal? Perhaps you haven't seen the Sunday papers?' Orbury handed his own copy to Aunt Ivy. 'Your Post Office "thief" had an alibi, after all, it seems. He'd only spent the night in the woods because he'd quarrelled with his wife. I see they've arrested the *Bugle* editor instead.'

'Wow! Let's have a look!' Jake began reading bits of the story out loud, while Lenny and Aunt Ivy listened in astonishment. '"I meant to return the stamps and postal orders in a day or two," Mr Grubb told the police. "I only did it to make some news. Nothing ever happens in Bottlecombe."'

Orbury grinned mysteriously at Jostling. 'If only he'd waited a bit longer, eh?'

It was roast chicken for lunch, preceded by delicious home-made vegetable soup and followed by perfect strawberry tart and cream. Jake and Lenny watched anxiously from the kitchen window in case the guests should want seconds, or even thirds, of strawberry tart, leaving none for them to have later. But all was well, and when the coffee was ready Miles invited Ivy and the boys to join them at the table.

By now, that Sunday had turned into a perfect summer's day. Even Ivy herself thought she had never seen the countryside looking lovelier. The garden was certainly at its best, all fresh and sparkling after the rain, and Ivy could not help feeling a little glow of pride as she glanced around.

Miles Pellington came straight to the point. 'My dear lady, we have a proposition to put to

73

you.' He was, it seemed, a programme produc-
er of the highest standing, and about to
embark upon a series called 'Ghost Garden'.
'Six programmes to start with, but if it proves
popular we can stretch to many more.' The
programme would be separate stories about

74

different uncanny dramas from the past, which
had all happened in or around the same country garden. With unrestrained enthusiasm
Miles concluded: 'And yours is the very garden
we've been looking for.'

Lenny and Jake sat frog-eyed, and it was

obvious that Aunt Ivy, too, had been taken completely by surprise. Her face changed colours like a scared chameleon, and she darted her anxious gaze from one man to another. 'What—what would I have to do?'

'Why, nothing, except hire us your garden— and keep on providing these wonderful meals for our cast.'

'Plus all the visitors you'll have when the series becomes famous,' Jostling added.

'Hey, that's terrific!' Lenny said at last. 'You'll be really rich, Aunt Ivy.'

'And famous,' added Jake, getting his priorities right.

'Yes—I suppose so,' Aunt Ivy whispered with a touch of regret. She had often wished the garden were more successful, but now, perversely, she could not help thinking of the trampling hordes destroying the peace of her bit of countryside. Then there was all that extra cooking, not to mention the washing-up. She would have to take on help, and help was not always what it should be these days. All the same, one must not be ungrateful. She smiled bravely round the table.

'I expect you've already planned the first six stories?' Lenny enquired. 'If not, I think I could help you. One story could be about this boy magician, who puts on a show in this ghost garden and finds he has really made his friend disappear in a trick called "The Vanishing Accomplice". There's this double fold in the curtain, and the friend's supposed to hide in that, but when he whisks it away . . . .'

Orbury laughed. 'A good try, Lenny, but Miles never works with dogs or children.' Lenny looked hurt.

'Pity. Especially since without me and Jake you'd never have found this place.'

'How do you make that out, Lenny? Don't forget we came here in response to a tip-off from the newspaper. . .'

'. . . telling you Dave Doyle had seen a UFO.'

'. . . which turned out to be a band-stand roof flying through the air.'

'No, that's where you're wrong. Dave had seen our umbrella.' Lenny felt that nobody would ever prove otherwise. 'Anyway, if we hadn't gone after the umbrella we'd never have found the Post Office loot, so you wouldn't have got your story.'

'And Mr Grubb would have sneaked the stuff back and maybe got away with it.'

Orbury admitted the truth of this, and pointed out that the stunning shots he had taken of the 'saucer' and surrounding countryside were the shots which had really caught Miles's interest.

'You see?' crowed Jake. 'In any case, Lenny was the one who thought of a ghost garden in the first place. The Haunted Ivy Tea Garden. He'd been planning it since last Wednesday.'

'And I've been planning it for a year and a half,' grinned Miles. 'Ask Jocelyn and Aubrey if you don't believe me.'

Lenny Hargreaves smiled a superior smile. 'I believe you,' he said generously. 'Great minds think alike.'

Hazel Townson

If you're an eager Beaver reader, perhaps you ought to try some more of our exciting and funny adventures by Hazel Townson. They are available in bookshops or they can be ordered directly from us. Just complete the form below and enclose the right amount of money and the books will be sent to you.

☐	THE BARLEY SUGAR GHOSTS	85p
☐	THE GREAT ICE-CREAM CRIME	£1.25
☐	THE SIEGE OF COBB STREET SCHOOL	95p
☐	THE VANISHING GRAN	£1.25
☐	THE SPECKLED PANIC	£1.25
☐	THE SHRIEKING FACE	£1.25
☐	HAUNTED IVY	£1.25

Postage _____

Total _____

And if you'd like to hear about NEW Hazel Townson titles and more about Beaver Books in general, don't forget to write and ask for our Beaver Bulletin. Just send a stamped, self-addressed envelope to Beaver Books, 62-5 Chandos Place, London WC2N 4NW and we will send you our latest one.

If you would like to order books, please send this form with the money due to:

BEAVER PAPERBACK CASH SALES, PO BOX 11, FALMOUTH, CORNWALL TR10 9EN.

Send a cheque or postal order, and don't forget to include postage at the following rates: UK: 55p for the first book, 22p for the second, 14p for each additional book; BFPO and Eire: 55p for the first book, 22p for the second, 14p for the next seven books and 8p per book thereafter. Overseas: £1.00 for the first book and 25p for each additional book.

NAME..

ADDRESS..

....

Please print clearly